Dear Parent:
Your child's love of readin

D1506669

Every child learns to read in a different way and at his or her own speed. You can help your young reader improve and become more confident by encouraging his or her own interests and abilities. You can also guide your child's spiritual development by reading stories with biblical values and Bible stories, like I Can Read! books published by Zonderkidz. From books your child reads with you to the first books he or she reads alone, there are I Can Read! books for every stage of reading:

 SHARED READING
Basic language, word repetition, and whimsical illustrations, ideal for sharing with your emergent reader.

 BEGINNING READING
Short sentences, familiar words, and simple concepts for children eager to read on their own.

 READING WITH HELP
Engaging stories, longer sentences, and language play for developing readers.

 READING ALONE
Complex plots, challenging vocabulary, and high-interest topics for the independent reader.

 ADVANCED READING
Short paragraphs, chapters, and exciting themes for the perfect bridge to chapter books.

I Can Read! books have introduced children to the joy of reading since 1957. Featuring award-winning authors and illustrators and a fabulous cast of beloved characters, I Can Read! books set the standard for beginning readers.

A lifetime of discovery begins with the magical words **"I Can Read!"**

Visit www.icanread.com for information on enriching your child's reading experience.
Visit www.zonderkidz.com for more Zonderkidz I Can Read! titles.

Shout to the LORD with joy, everyone on earth.
—*Psalm 100:1*

What Do I See?
Copyright © 2000, 2008 by Crystal Bowman
Illustrations copyright © 2000 by Pam Thomson

Requests for information should be addressed to:
Zonderkidz, Grand Rapids, Michigan 49530

Library of Congress Cataloging-in-Publication Data
Bowman, Crystal.
   What do I see? / story by Crystal Bowman ; pictures by Pam Thomson.
     p. cm. -- (I can read! Level 1)
   Previously published in different form under title: See the country, see the city.
   Summary: A walk through the country and the city introduces mooing cows, waddling
ducks, beeping cars, and friendly policemen.
   ISBN-13: 978-0-310-71573-3 (softcover)
   ISBN-10: 0-310-71573-3 (softcover)
   [1. Country life--Fiction. 2. City and town life--Fiction. 3. Sound--Fiction. 4. Christian
life--Fiction.] I. Thomson, Pam, ill. II. Title.
   PZ7.B6834Wh 2008
   [E]--dc22
2007023153

Zonderkidz is a trademark of Zondervan.

Art Direction: Jody Langley
Cover Design: Sarah Molegraaf

Printed in China

08 09 10 • 4 3 2 1

I Can Read! ™

BEGINNING 1 READING

Slatington Library

What Do I See?

story by Crystal Bowman

pictures by Pam Thomson

4

I walk in the country.

What do I see?

I see a fuzzy bumblebee.

I see a toad

by the side of the road.

I see a cow who moos at me.

Moo, moo, cow.

Hop, hop, toad.

Buzz, buzz, fuzzy bumblebee.

I walk in the country.

What do I see?

I see a happy apple tree.

I see a hill

and a church with a bell.

I see God's sun that shines on me.

Shine, shine, sun.

Ring, ring, bell.

Be happy, happy apple tree.

I walk in the country.

What do I see?

I see fishes, one, two, three.

I see a worm who likes to squirm.

I see a duck who quacks at me.

Quack, quack, duck.

Squirm, squirm, worm.

Swim, swim, fishes, one, two, three.

I come back from the country.

What do I see?

I see my house.

It's waiting for me.

I walk in the city.

What do I see?

I see a blackbird up in the tree.

I see two cats
asleep on a mat.

I see a car that beeps at me.

Beep, beep, car.

Sleep, sleep, cats.

Chirp, chirp, blackbird
up in the tree.

I walk in the city.

What do I see?

I see tall buildings,

one, two, three.

I see God's rainbow in the sky.

I see a light that blinks at me.

Blink, blink, light.

Glow, glow, rainbow.

Stand tall buildings,

one, two, three.

I walk in the city.

What do I see?

I see people on a shopping spree.

I see a bus that zooms by us.

I see a policeman who says hi to me.

Hello, policeman.

Zoom, zoom, bus.

Shop, shop, people

on a shopping spree.

I come back from the city.

What do I see?

I see my house.

It's waiting for me.

Thank you, God, for all I see:

the church, the sun,

and the apple tree.